This Book Belongs To:

.............................................................................

.............................................................................

Originally published as *Albert Megavoet* in Belgium and the Netherlands by Clavis Uitgeverij, 2020
English translation from the Dutch by Clavis Publishing Inc., New York

Visit us on the Web at www.clavis-publishing.com.

*Extraordinary Albert* written by Bonnie Grubman and illustrated by S.K.Y. van der Wel

ISBN 978-1-60537-592-2

This book was printed in December 2020 at Nikara, M. R. Štefánika 858/25, 963 01 Krupina, Slovakia.

First Edition
10 9 8 7 6 5 4 3 2 1

Clavis Publishing supports the First Amendment and celebrates the right to read.

*For Albert—*

# EXTRAORDINARY
# ALBERT

WRITTEN BY
BONNIE GRUBMAN
ILLUSTRATED BY
S.K.Y. VAN DER WEL

Clavis
NEW YORK

*♡ Extraordinary You!*
*♡ Bonnie Grubman*

On the day Albert was born his parents cried out: "He's here!"

"He's a dream come true," gushed his mother.

"Yes he is," said his father.

And they kissed their son from head to toe.

"He's positively perfect," said his mother.

"With extraordinary feet," gloated his father.

Albert loved his feet, and grew into a happy, healthy,
bouncing baby gorilla.

He clapped.
Played patty-cake.

Waved bye-bye.

Mastered standing without toppling.

And used his feet to his advantage.

But when Albert got big enough to appreciate his unique feet; he didn't. He hated them. He tripped over them more times than he liked to admit. His custom-made cleats took up too much room in his closet and the one-size-fits-all socks didn't include him.

"Why can't I have perfect feet like Rex?" whimpered Albert.

"Oh Albert, dear. Your feet *are* perfect. Other animals would wish for feet like yours."

Albert knew his mom would say that. He also didn't believe it for one minute.

"I can't even tiptoe without shaking the ground,
or dance without stepping on someone. Gosh.
I can't even kick a soccer ball without breaking a window.
What reasonable animal would want to have feet like *mine*?"

One day, Albert and Rex
were playing hide and seek.
"I'll count, you hide, Albert."
Albert ran behind a big rock.
"Ready or not, here I come!" called Rex.

But as soon as Rex opened his eyes, he saw Albert hiding in plain sight. "I don't think I'm cut out for this," he moped.

So they played leapfrog instead.
Jumping was easy for Albert.
Stooping was not.
No matter how hard he tried,
his feet always got in the way.

"I have a great idea," said Rex.
"Let's go to the playground."
So off they went.

Along the dirt path,
under the boughs,
across the shallow creek,
whistling and singing, until . . .

Albert's foot got tangled in the tall grass.

"I'm sorry, Rex. I'm such a bother."

"Not to me," said Rex.

"I hate my feet times a hundred."

"You shouldn't, Albert. They're extraordinary."

"That's what my Dad says."

Tears welled up in Albert's eyes, and he wiped his cheek.

"Are you crying, Albert?"

"No. I just felt a raindrop."

And just like that, the heavens opened. The rain fell hard and fast, and thunder rolled across the sky like a bowling ball.

"I'm scared. Very, very scared," moaned Rex.
Albert wrapped his arms and feet around Rex.
"Th-thanks, Albert," said Rex. "I feel better now."

Soon after, the rain slackened. But as it did, dark clouds loomed in the distance. "I think we should head home before it comes down again," said Albert. "Which way do we go?" asked Rex.

"We follow our footprints."

"But didn't the rain wash them away?"

"Not all of them," said Albert.

Albert and Rex made an about-face and retraced Albert's trail of footprints.

Through the tall grass, across the shallow creek,
under the boughs, and along the dirt path.

"Told you, Albert."
"Told me what, Rex?"
"Your feet are extraordinary. I wish I had feet
like *yours*. You're my hero, Albert. My best friend."

The next morning,
Albert and Rex met up at the park.
"You're it!" tagged Albert.
And when Albert's feet got in the way,
he didn't mind very much at all.